HAZEL VALLEY SCHOOL

# SCREEN of FROGS

A Richard Jackson Book

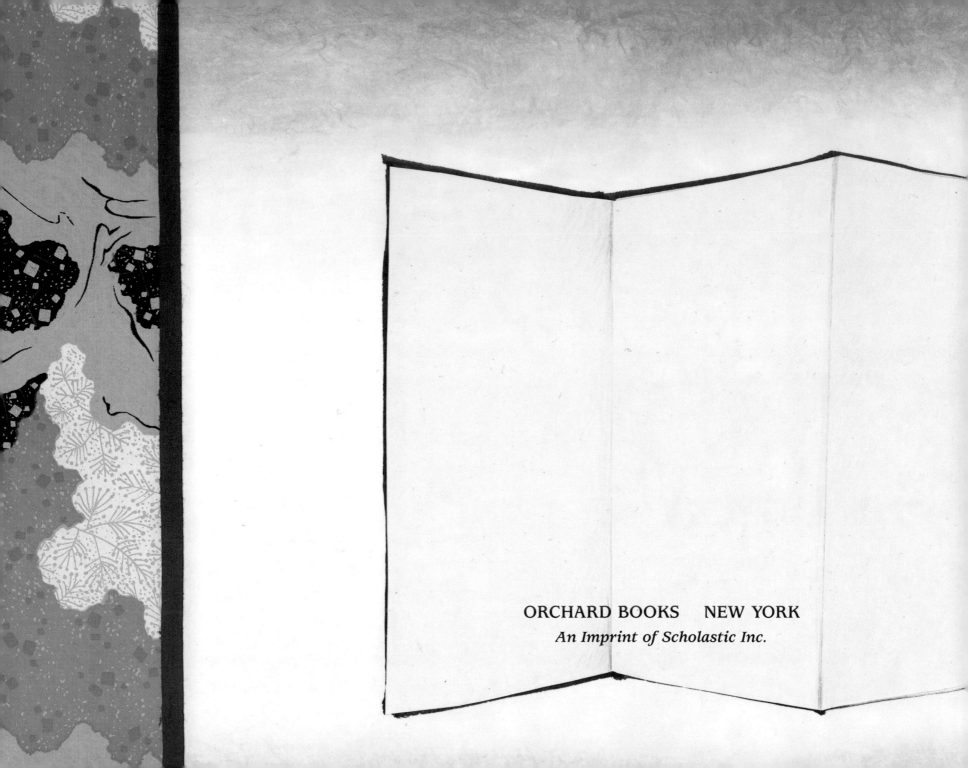

ORCHARD BOOKS    NEW YORK

*An Imprint of Scholastic Inc.*

# SCREEN of FROGS

### An Old Tale Retold and Illustrated by

## Sheila Hamanaka

The text is adapted from "The Strange Folding Screen," a story in *Nihon No Minwa,*
edited by Minori Kakiuchi, published by Mirai-Sha, Tokyo, Japan.

Library of Congress Cataloging-in-Publication Data
Hamanaka, Sheila.
Screen of frogs : an old tale / retold and illustrated by Sheila Hamanaka.    p.   cm.
"A Richard Jackson book"—P.
Summary: A spoiled rich man in Japan discovers a respect for nature in time
to turn his life around.
ISBN 0-531-05464-0
[1. Folklore—Japan.]   I. Title. PZ8.1.H149Sc   1993   398.21—dc20   [E]   92-24172

10 9 8 7 6 5 4 3

Printed in Mexico   49
Book design by Mina Greenstein
The text of this book is set in 16 point Usherwood Medium. The illustrations are
acrylic and collage on handmade kozo paper, reproduced in full color.

To the memory of my grandfather,
Koji Sasaki

Long ago in Japan there lived a wealthy boy named Koji. For as far as the eye could see, the fields and lakes and mountains belonged to Koji's family. From his great house he saw the peasants working from sunup to sundown. They gave all the rice they grew to his parents, while they themselves ate only millet and barley.

"Ha!" said Koji. "Working is for fools! Look, they work all day and still they're as poor as field mice! I'll never work!"

The lazy boy grew into a lazy man. After his parents died, Koji began selling off the fields and lakes and mountains one after the other. He needed money and had no time to manage the land, he was so busy lying by the stream watching the cherry blossoms float by . . . or gazing at the moon . . .

. . . or buying whatever he pleased—horses and dogs
and hunting falcons, rare silks and scrolls
and painted screens.

Years passed, and Koji needed more and more money to pay his debts. Finally, he had only his great house and one mountain and a lake left.

"Oh, well." He sighed. "It seems I have no choice." So he set off to measure what little remained of his estate.

Koji found it hard work measuring the land step by step and counting all those valuable trees. He was not used to working. When he came to his favorite lake at the foot of the mountain, Koji decided to take a nap.

As he drifted toward sleep, he thought he saw a beautiful woman dressed in a green kimono tiptoeing across the lily pads. He smiled and closed his eyes because he knew he must be dreaming.

Suddenly, a huge, wet, green hand grabbed his foot! It wasn't a woman but a frog—as large as a man and dressed in dripping green weeds.

"Oh, pardon me," said the frog. "I didn't mean to scare you. But aren't you Koji, who used to come here as a little boy?"

Koji trembled and opened his mouth, but no words came out. He nodded yes.

"Well, the bees told the birds and the birds told the fox and the fox told the trees and the trees told the bees—I mean, the trees told the water lilies and the water lilies told us that you've sold all the fields and forests for as far as the eye can see and now you're about to sell this mountain. Is that true?"

Yes, nodded Koji.

"Oh, *no! No! No! No! No!*" cried the frog. "You see, if you sell the mountain, the woodcutters will chop down all the trees and the bees and the birds and the fox will have no place to live, and the sun will dry out the soil and the rains will wash the earth into the streams and lakes, filling them up, and then we'll all be homeless, too!" Great tears welled in the frog's eyes. "Please, please, don't sell this land!" the frog sobbed.

Koji turned to look at the beautiful mountainside, but as he did so he heard a loud *PLOP!* The frog was gone.

"It's just a bad dream, a nightmare," Koji said to himself. "I must be working too hard." And he fled all the way home, feeling the eyes of a thousand forest creatures on his back.

Troubled and anxious, Koji decided to keep the land. He paid off his debts instead by selling his furniture and screens and scrolls and horses and dogs and hunting falcons, and even his gold statues of Buddha.

At last he had nothing but the futon he slept on and an old, worthless, blank folding screen. The great empty house creaked, but Koji fell asleep happy, thinking about the frogs and all the other creatures he had spared.

In the middle of the night Koji's eyes suddenly popped open. He heard something. . . .

"*Kero-kero-kero.*" Why, it sounded like small frogs chirping!

"*Gero-gero-gero.*" And big frogs croaking! The chirps and croaks grew louder and louder. . . .

"KERO-KERO-KERO!"
"GERO-GERO-GERO!"
Koji leaped out of bed. Nothing! But . . .
there were hundreds of wet frog prints on the
floor! He followed them.

"The screen!" he shouted when he saw it.
The old blank screen was covered with
pictures of frogs. And the paint was still wet.
Frogs! Big frogs, little frogs, brown and gold
and green frogs.
Koji fell back, amazed.

Soon word spread, and all his neighbors and then the whole village came to see the screen. Lords, peasants, samurai and sword smiths, noodle makers, koto players, glassblowers, umbrella makers. And all their children, too.

"Why, the frogs look alive!"

"This one is painted with only two strokes!"

"It's a masterpiece! I'll buy it!"

"No! Let me buy it!"

But to everyone Koji said, "No, thank you." And from that day he began to work hard. The neighboring peasants showed him how to grow rice and millet and barley and vegetables in his garden. No one could make him part with his land or the screen, no matter how much they offered.

Soon Koji married. His wife and children helped him work in the fields and around the house. He often took his family to the lake to admire the frogs and the mountainside.

One day, after many years,
Koji died. That night
something strange happened.
The painted frogs began to
fade. By the next morning
the screen was blank!

Koji's family held the land for generations. And today, long after the screen has crumbled away, frogs are still croaking and swimming in the mountain lake.